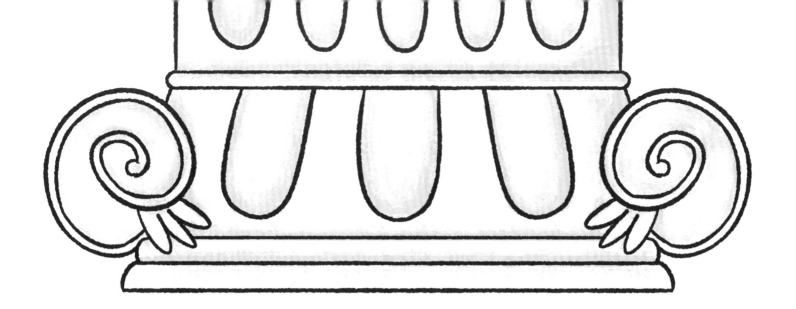

SCHOOL OF GREATNESS

THE MISSING MASCOT:
HERCULES' STORY ABOUT TEAMWORK

For my brother, who shares my love of reading and writing and has always been one of the best members of my team!
– KK

You can acomplish so much with the right team!
– GB

Genius Cat Books

 Genius Cat

www.geniuscatbooks.com

Parkland, FL

ABOUT THIS BOOK
The art for this book was created with photoshop and illustrator, using a Wacom Cintiq. Text was set in Forma DJR Micro, Copperplate, and Impetus. It was designed by Germán Blanco.

Library of Congress Control Number: 2022933497

ISBN: 978-1-938447-30-3 (hardcover)

First edition, 2022

Our books may be purchased in bulk for promotional, educational, or business use. For more information, or to schedule an event, please visit geniuscatbooks.com.

Printed and bound in China.

CHARACTER PRONUNCIATION GUIDE

 Achilles: *Uh · Kill · Eez*

 **Cerberus |** *Sir · Burr · Us*

 Circe: *Sir · See (or Sirs)*

 Cyclops: *Sigh · Klops*

 Hercules: *Her · Q · Leez*

 **Medusa:** *Muh · Doo · Suh*

 **Midas |** *My · Dus*

 Minotaur | *Min · Uh · Tore*

 Pandora | *Pan · Door · Uh*

Ms. Pythia | *Pith · Ee · Uh*
(but you can call her Ms. P!)

"Good morning class!" said Ms. Pythia (or Ms. P, for short).
"Today we're learning about—"

Ms. P was suddenly interrupted by a school announcement.

"Alert! Cerberus is on the loose!," said Mr. K, the school messenger. "Repeat, our school mascot has escaped. We need a hero to find him and return him to his cave. Volunteer if you dare!"

Hercules jumped to his feet.
"I'll be the hero, Ms. P!" he said.
"I can catch Cerberus."

Ms. P wrote Hercules a hall pass.
"You can try," she said. "As long as
you bring a buddy with you."

"I don't need help!" Hercules
replied.

But since Ms. P wouldn't let him
leave without a buddy, Hercules
chose Cyclops.

"He's the strongest," said
Hercules. "After me, of course."

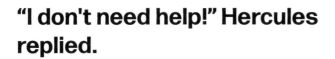

Hercules and Cyclops wandered through the halls searching for Cerberus. They followed some clues to the cafeteria, where they saw…

"Cerberus!" Hercules exclaimed.

"Don't get in the way!" Hercules told Cyclops before taking off after Cerberus.

But Cerberus was too fast and dashed out the door before Hercules could reach him!

"Now what?" asked Cyclops, trying to catch his breath.

Hercules grabbed some food. "We'll set a trap!" he said.

Hercules and Cyclops set the trap and hid behind the school fountain.

"Can I hold the rope?" asked Cyclops.

"No!" shouted Hercules. "This is *my* task. I need to be the one to catch Cerberus."

While Hercules and Cyclops argued, Cerberus grabbed the food and escaped!

"You should've stopped him!" said Hercules.

Cyclops narrowed his eye. "I didn't see *you* stopping him either," Cyclops replied.

"I need a new buddy," Hercules said.

Back in the classroom, Hercules looked for another buddy. He wanted someone fast, so he chose Achilles. Maybe if Cyclops had been faster, they would have caught Cerberus.

"Cerberus is no match for my strength and your speed together!" Hercules declared.

"I'm as fast as a chariot!" said Achilles.

As soon as they stepped into the hallway, Cerberus sped by. He was chasing Sisypuss, the school cat.

WOOF
WOOF

With lightning speed, Achilles cornered Cerberus at the end of the hallway. "He's trapped!" Achilles yelled.

"And now I'll catch him,"
said Hercules.

"I'll get him!" said Achilles.
"I'm faster!"

Hercules pushed
Achilles out of the way.
"It's *my* task," he said.

But when Hercules bent to pick
up Cerberus, he slipped through
Hercules's legs and ran away!

Achilles watched Cerberus disappear. "Well, I tried," Achilles said.

"But we can't stop until we complete the task!" Hercules said.

"Since it's *your* task, I'm going back to class," Achilles replied.

Back in class, Hercules wondered if he would ever complete his task. What was he doing wrong? If he didn't catch Cerberus, he would never become a hero!

Circe noticed that Hercules was upset, and decided to help.

"You're never going to *catch* Cerberus," Circe told Hercules. "But I might have an idea of how we can get him back to his cave!"

"Tell me your idea," said Hercules, "and I'll make sure Cerberus doesn't get away this time!"

Hercules and Circe found Cerberus in the library. "Let's see if he wants to play," Circe said, throwing some balls from her pocket across the room. Cerberus happily ran to the balls and brought them back to her.

"Oh!" exclaimed Hercules, watching Circe play with Cerberus. "Instead of us chasing him, we can have him chase the balls!"

Circe led Cerberus down the hallway, past the fountain, and all the way to his cave. Hercules followed behind them, not feeling very heroic.

But when Circe got to Cerberus's cave, she couldn't close the heavy gate.

"I can do it!" said Hercules, seeing his chance to help.

Circe moved out of the way as Hercules pushed and pushed, until the gate finally closed.

"We did it!" they shouted.

Hercules and Circe returned to class victorious.

"I completed the task, just like I said I would." said Hercules.
"I'm a hero!"

"Hmmm," said Ms. P. "I think it's time to consult the scrolls."

"Responsibility," Ms. P read.
"No, that's not it."

"Honesty? Not this
one, either."

"Oh yes, here we go: teamwork!"
Ms. P exclaimed.

Ms. P read the scroll out loud to her class.

TEAMWORK

Teamwork is when you work together.

Everyone has a role.

Do your best and support each other,

And the team will reach its goal!

"Do you think you were a good teammate on your task to catch Cerberus, Hercules?" asked Ms. P.

"He got mad at me when Cerberus escaped, but it wasn't even my fault," Cyclops said.

"Then he pushed me out of the way so he could grab Cerberus by himself!" Achilles added.

"It's true," said Hercules. "I guess I wasn't a great teammate *or* a good hero. I'm sorry."

"But you learned," said Circe. "You let me help—and then you helped me, too."

"Sounds like teamwork to me!" said Ms. P.

"Now let's work together to clean up the mess Cerberus made," said Ms. P, "because with teamwork, we can accomplish any task!"

Then everyone in Ms. P's class decided to take the Teamwork Pledge so they would always remember that they are stronger together.

TEAMWORK PLEDGE

I'll work hard and do my part,
And I'll support my teammates, too.
I pledge to listen, learn, and work together,
So there'll be no stopping what we can do!

HERCULES

Heracles (better known by his Roman name, Hercules) is one of the greatest heroes in Greek Mythology, known for his amazing strength and courage. Hercules was half human, half god. His mother was a mortal, but his father was the king of all gods, Zeus. According to legend, Zeus's wife, Hera, did not like Hercules and tricked him into hurting his family. Even though it wasn't his fault, Hercules felt guilty about what happened. A king gave Hercules 12 almost-impossible tasks to complete to make up for what he had done. His final task was to bring back the 3-headed guard dog, Cerberus, from the Underworld.

Hercules spent most of his life completing his 12 tasks and ridding the ancient Greek world of monsters. But he usually wasn't alone. He had volunteers and friends with him on his journeys. While he may have been a hero, even Hercules knew he needed a team to accomplish his goals!

CERBERUS

In Greek mythology, Cerberus is the watchdog who guarded the gates of the Underworld. Cerberus was caught by Hercules in his twelfth and final task.

Print your own Teamwork Pledge at **geniuscatbooks.com**!
@geniuscatbooks